ENDORSEMENTS

"I'm ready to pull up a chair in The Sweet Shop, savor a slice of cinnamon bread, and dig into this juicy mystery."

~ DANA MENTINK – MULTI PUBLISHED, AWARD WINNING AUTHOR

"A sweet, fun and intriguing mystery you can really sink your teeth into."

~ RACHEL L MILLER - AUTHOR OF THE AMISH ROMANCE SERIES: *WINDY GAP WISHES*

"I feel as if I know these characters, have walked down these streets, went along for the *"ride"* with Katie while she solved this mystery. Don't miss it!!"

~ JC MORROWS – BESTSELLING AUTHOR OF THE YA SERIES: *ORDER OF THE MOONSTONE*

BLUEBERRY CUPCAKE MYSTERY

BOOKS BY NAOMI MILLER

BLUEBERRY CUPCAKE MYSTERY

CHRISTMAS COOKIE MYSTERY
(COMING SOON)

AMISH SWEET SHOP
MYSTERY

BLUEBERRY CUPCAKE MYSTERY

BY
NAOMI MILLER

Blueberry Cupcake Mystery
Copyright © 2016 by Naomi Miller

Blueberry Cupcake Mystery / Naomi Miller

ISBN: 978-0692701379   (Paperback)
ISBN: 978-0692686294   (Paperback)
ISBN: 978-1533793140   (E-BOOK)
ASIN: B01E3A1ATC   (KINDLE)

1. Books / Mystery, Thriller & Suspense / Mystery / Cozy
/ Culinary. 2. Books / Teen & Young Adult / Literature &
Fiction / Religious / Christian / Mysteries & Thrillers.
3. Teen & Young Adult / Literature & Fiction / Religious.
4. Teen & Young Adult / Religion & Spirituality.   5.
Fiction / Christian Books & Bibles / Literature &
Fiction / Amish & Mennonite.

LOC: 2016938044

S&G Publishing, Knoxville, TN
www.sgpublish.com

Cover design © Rachel L. Miller (S&G Publishing)

First Edition 2016

To God be the Glory...

A NOTE FROM NAOMI MILLER

I love reading Amish fiction! I feel the Lord is calling me to write Amish fiction that is fun to read; free from the usual stress, anxiety, and other stomach-tightening reactions. Instead, I'm hoping to instill good feelings, good emotions, and good reactions.

I have created fictional characters, in a fictional town. As with any work of fiction, I've taken license in some areas of research as a means of creating circumstances necessary to my characters or plot. Any inaccuracies in the Amish, Mennonite or English lifestyles portrayed in this book are completely due to fictional license.

God bless you!

~Naomi

GLOSSARY

The German/Dutch dialect spoken by the Amish is not a written language. It is solely dependent on the location and origin of each settlement. The spellings below are approximations.

allrecht = all right

appeditlich = delicious

bruder/bruders = brother/brothers

buwe/buwes = boy/boys

danki = thank you

dat = dad

dochder = daughter

du bischt daheem = you're home

Englischer = non-Amish person

freind/freinden = friend/friends

gen gschehne = you're welcome

Gott = God

jah = yes

kaffe = coffee

kumme = come

maedel/maedels = girl/girls

mamm = mom

naerfich = nervous

nee = no

rumschpringe = running around time for youth

schweschder = sister

wunderbaar = wonderful

And be ye kind one to another, tenderhearted, forgiving one another, even as God for Christ's sake hath forgiven you.

Ephesians 4:32

For Rachel

ONE

Katie Chupp felt a chill run through her as she unlocked the door to The Sweet Shop. Hesitating, she turned and looked around, taking in the scenery around her.

It didn't seem possible that the feeling had anything to do with her surroundings. The day was just beginning and it looked as if it was going to be a beautiful day.

The blue sky was pleasant to behold, with white, fluffy clouds lazily floating by, the sun already shining brightly, and a warm breeze gently wafting around her.

Katie was glad Mrs. Simpkins didn't ask her employees to come in earlier than six o'clock. It was a rare morning that Katie would arrive at work before sunrise.

Up and down the street, American flags were waving in the breeze, heralding the festivities. Red, white and blue decorations were in all the store windows. The town was ready to celebrate Independence Day.

Katie anxiously awaited the fireworks that would be set off tonight, under cover of darkness. She was looking forward to sitting on a blanket with her family, watching as the fireworks exploded high in the sky.

The Fourth of July was one of her favorite holidays. Everyone met at the town square to celebrate. Many of the families, including Katie's, would eat a late supper while waiting for the fireworks.

Katie always had such a *gut* time. Her *freinden*, Freida and Anna would sit with her and they would all chat incessantly.

Freida usually chatted about the *buwes* in the community; somehow she always knew which *buwes* and *maedels* were courting—or thinking about it.

Katie had no time to waste—yet she waited, sensing that something was wrong. She couldn't imagine what it could be, to cause such a reaction. It made no sense to her.

The Sweet Shop would be busy today. Extra baking had been done during the past few days, in preparation of the holiday. Lots of customers would be coming into the bakery to pick up their orders today.

Katie-girl, you need to stop this nonsense and get to work. You don't have time to waste. You have a lot to do before customers begin showing up.

Her thoughts shifted to the long list of tasks that must be completed each day to prepare for customers. There was much to be done. There would be no time to rest once the bakery opened.

With a silent prayer of thanks for such a beautiful day, Katie stepped inside the bakery.

Uttering a cry of alarm, Katie collided with the door as she involuntarily stepped back.

The bakery was a mess!

The glass in the display case provided a clear view of the disaster awaiting her. The shelves were mostly empty; all the special treats created just for the holiday were gone! All that was left behind were broken pieces of decoration . . . and a few crumbs.

There is nothing worth keeping. Nothing.

Looking around, Katie noticed that the jars of jam, preserves, butters and specialty items were somewhat intact, although a few had fallen—or been knocked—to the floor.

But the pretty rows of bread . . . dozens of loaves looked to be missing, especially the pumpkin, cinnamon, and zucchini bread.

It looked as if the lower shelves had taken the brunt of the damage, while most of the items on the higher shelves had been left alone.

Why? Why would someone take so much from the lower shelves and leave the top shelves pretty much alone? That makes no sense. Who would do such a thing?

Katie didn't know what to do next. Mrs. Simpkins didn't arrive for another hour, but she would need to be told.

As soon as possible.

Dear Gott, I'm scared! Give me wisdom to know what to do and the courage to do it. Tell me—

A loud rapping at the door startled her, causing her to jump back, once again hitting the door.

"Katie, what are you doing in there? Why are you blocking the door? Katie Chupp, you let me in this instant."

Taking a shaky breath, Katie turned away from the mess, opening the door and then moving through it before her *freind* could step through the doorway—into the bakery—and the same scene Katie had just discovered.

Freida Schmidt, Katie's *freind* and co-worker, was standing outside, impatiently waiting to enter the bakery. She normally arrived about thirty minutes after Katie. It was likely that she came early this morning, being excited about the holiday celebration tonight and wanting to chat before the others arrived.

"Freida, I'm for sure glad to see you. You are not going to believe what's happened!"

Katie's words rushed out quickly. "Just take a look in the window. But do not go inside."

As Katie moved away from the doorway, a look of shock appeared on the face of her *freind*, before she had even taken a step toward the room.

"*Ach*, Katie! What is going on? Who would do such a thing? It's ruined!" Freida looked as if she might drop down in a heap.

"Freida, maybe you should sit down, but not inside the bakery. I need to call Mrs. Simpkins and tell her what has happened. She will know what to do next. Are you going to be okay until I get back?"

"Get back? Get back? What do you mean? Where are you going?"

"Um . . . I'm thinking I might run over to The Coffee Cup. I am not about to go back into the bakery to call Mrs. Simpkins. Whoever did this might still be inside. It's not safe."

"Then you are not leaving me here alone.

If you're going, I'm going with you."

"*Allrecht.* Just let me lock the door, so no one else can get in until we get back." Moving past her *freind*, Katie placed her key into the lock for the second time that morning. She turned it until she heard a click. Then she placed the key in her pocket and turned back to her *freind*, before putting her arm around Freida.

"Let's go, then. I won't be going back in there anytime soon. After I call Mrs. Simpkins, we can return to wait for her. But we'll be waiting outside the bakery—not inside."

"Or maybe you could tell Mrs. Simpkins we will be waiting at one of the tables outside The Coffee Cup? Wouldn't that be a better idea?"

Katie only nodded her head as they crossed the street, looking carefully down each side in the early morning light.

A cup of kaffe would be a gut idea.

At the very least, it might help with the shaking that had taken hold of her hands.

TWO

Katie suggested Freida sit at one of the outdoor tables in front of the coffee shop across the street from the bakery.

Although it was going to be a hot day, there was a breeze blowing. Besides, Katie felt a bit of a chill—and had ever since she had opened the bakery door earlier.

Once Freida was settled, Katie stepped up to the front door and was relieved to see her *freind* Hannah at the counter.

The Coffee Cup would not open for another half hour, but Katie was certain Hannah would allow her to come in and use the phone.

Especially when she finds out why...

When she knocked on the glass door, Hannah looked up. Seeing Katie, she quickly came around the counter and unlocked the door, before opening it.

"Katie! What are you doing here at this hour? Why are you not already doing your baking?"

"Hannah, you are not going to believe what happened! Just let me call Mrs. Simpkins first, and I will tell you about it."

"You are welcome to use the phone. But why do you not use the one at The Sweet Shop?"

"I will tell you, but first, let me call Mrs.

Simpkins. She needs to know what has happened." Katie walked over to the telephone on the counter.

After dialing Mrs. Simpkins' number, she turned to Hannah, with her first finger at her lips.

Katie's boss, Amelia Simpkins, must have been near the phone, because she answered after the first ring.

"Hello."

"Hello, Mrs. Simpkins. This is Katie Chupp. There is a problem at The Sweet Shop. We have had a break-in. When I got there this morning, everything was a mess." Katie's voice shook, but she bravely continued, knowing that she needed to give Mrs. Simpkins the information she needed.

"Oh, my goodness! Are you all right? Was anyone there when you arrived? Was anything taken?"

"They took everything that was in the display case, plus a lot of the bread and stuff on the shelves. I didn't stay very long. I knew I would need to let you know about it as soon as possible. I don't know what the workroom looks like or if they took any—or all—of the orders we had prepared for the customers."

"My goodness! And where are you now, Katie? Are you at the bakery?"

"No, ma'am. I thought it best not to stay in the bakery. For one thing, I didn't know if someone might still be there, hiding. And, I thought you might need to notify the police and I didn't want to touch anything. I figured it was best to leave it just as I found it."

"That is very good thinking on your part. Yes, I think it is best that I go ahead and call the police department and have an officer meet us at the bakery. Where did you say you were calling from?"

"I'm sorry, Mrs. Simpkins. I forgot to tell you. I locked up and came straight to The Coffee Cup. I knew Hannah would be here early and she would let me use the telephone." Katie hesitated, before going on.

"I should also let you know, that Freida is here with me. She arrived just after I discovered the mess at the bakery. But I didn't really give her a chance to go in. As soon as she arrived, I came out and locked up, then we both came here—to The Coffee Cup. *Ach*, I am sorry. I think I am repeating myself. I am just so *naerfich*."

"It's all right, Katie. It's perfectly understandable for you to be shaken up over this. I don't know if I would be handling it as well as you are, if it had happened to me."

"Mrs. Simpkins, do you want us to go back to The Sweet Shop—or can we stay here until you arrive?"

"Well, for now, I think you should stay just where you are. I will meet you there—and tell the police where to find us. Then we can go over to the bakery together."

"Yes, Ma'am. That's just what we'll do. Thank you, Ma'am. Goodbye."

Hannah watched as Katie hung up the phone. When she turned to look her way, Hannah saw fear in her eyes. Hannah wondered what she could possibly do to help her *freind*.

Thank you, Gott. I am so blessed that I have never had to deal with a break-in. I never realized how scary it could be for the person it happens to. And thank you for taking care of my freinden.

Wondering what might help the *maedels*, she had an inspiration.

"Katie, could I make you a cup of strong, hot *kaffe*, with three lumps of sugar? I know that's the way you like it." Hannah had heard that sugar was sometimes helpful when someone had received a shock. Maybe it would help to lift Katie's spirits.

"*Ach*, that sounds *wunderbaar*, Hannah.

Could you please make one for Freida, too? She's just outside—at the table, waiting for me."

"Of course, I will. I know Freida likes lots of sugar in her *kaffe*. Should I add three lumps of sugar to her *kaffe*, too—or just bring the sugar bowl to the table?"

"That's probably a *gut* idea. You know how much Freida loves sweet stuff . . . drinks, pastries—even her breads end up sweeter when she bakes! Mrs. Simpkins usually assigns her the pastries at the bakery."

"I used to be surprised by how much sugar she adds to her *kaffe*. But *nee* one really cares, because she's such a sweet *maedel*."

"That is true."

"I have just brewed a fresh pot of *kaffe*. Why don't you join Freida outside at the table and I'll bring it out to you."

Hannah watched as Katie slowly moved

outside to one of the little tables. A few minutes later, she stepped outside, carrying a tray with three cups of delicious-smelling *kaffe*, along with two raspberry turnovers."

"I feel silly, bringing you pastries, but I figured you hadn't stopped for breakfast yet, and it goes so well with the *kaffe*. More than a third of the people who *kumme* in for *kaffe* also order some sort of pastry to go with it, I reckon."

"But listen to me go on . . . Katie, do tell us what happened this morning at the bakery. What brought you to The Coffee Cup so early?"

"Well, I don't know how much I should say about it, until Mrs. Simpkins and the police arrive, but I can tell you what I found. First, let us give thanks for this *gut* food."

After taking time for prayer, Katie took a bite of her turnover.

"This is *appeditlich*, Hannah. Freida, you need to try yours." Taking a sip of her *kaffe*,

Katie began answering their questions, starting at the beginning.

"I opened the shop at the usual time. It was when I stepped inside, that I looked up and saw everything was a huge mess!"

Hannah watched as Katie spoke about the break-in. Now that she was remembering the scene she had walked in on, she was looking more and more *naerfich*. Hannah hoped she wasn't going into shock. She was glad now, that she had thought to give them both hot *kaffe* with plenty of sugar.

"The display case was empty, except for crumbs and broken pieces of decorations. Much of the specialty breads were gone off the shelves. The only thing that wasn't so bad, were the jams and preserves and condiments.

Some were gone, *jah*, but much of them were right on the shelves, just as they were left last night."

"But Katie, I don't understand. What

could have happened?"

"I don't know, Hannah. I really don't know. I worried that whoever did it might still be lingering in the shop, so I hurried outside, locked the door tight, and came here with Freida. I didn't want to take a chance and stay in there another moment."

"But who could have done such a thing?" Freida finally found her voice. "Mrs. Simpkins is just the nicest person to work for. I don't know why anyone would do anything to hurt her."

"Well, but maybe it was a stranger." Katie answered her. "There are lots of visitors in town right now, with the holiday approaching and all the shops are having special sales to celebrate."

Hannah leaned across the table and said, in a low voice. "And why did you tell Mrs. Simpkins she needed to contact the police?"

Katie blew out a breath. "I know she has to report anything that happens at the bakery to her insurance company. I was certain they would insist on the police investigating the break-in."

"I would love to sit with you until Mrs. Simpkins arrives, but I had better get back inside and get everything ready for the customers who will be showing up here soon." With that, Hannah began to gather up the now-empty cups, along with the napkins and tray.

"*Danki* for the hot *kaffe* and fresh pastry." Katie smiled up at Hannah. "It's just what I needed to calm myself before going back to the bakery.

"*Danki* for thinking of me, too." Freida spoke, as Hannah stepped away from the little table.

"*Gen gschehne.* I'm so glad to be helpful on such a terrible morning." With that, Hannah excused herself and returned to the coffee shop.

After Hannah had gone back into the coffee shop, Katie looked over at Freida. "Hannah is a *gut freind. Jah?*"

"*Jah.* And you are truly a *gut freind*, too, Katie. I shudder to think of how close I came to walking into the mess at The Sweet Shop this morning. *Danki*, Katie-girl, for stopping me just in time." Freida looked so relieved, Katie almost laughed.

"Freida, I cannot stop thinking about how strange it all was. Do you really suppose it was a stranger? For sure and for certain, it couldn't have been anyone we know, could it?" Katie asked, before adding a personal thought.

"I'm thinking it must have been an *Englischer* . . . at least I hope so. I know that doesn't sound so *gut*, but I guess I just don't want to think that it could have been an Amish *freind*."

"I don't know, Katie. You know very well that some of the *buwes* go a little crazy on their *rumschpringe*. My *bruders* have come home smelling like cigarette smoke and alcohol." Freida looked outraged at the very thought of it.

"They even wore strange, *Englischer* clothes and rode around in fast cars. I heard that some of the *buwes* even carried cellphones around, but I don't think my *bruders* ever did. My *dat* would have had a fit."

At that moment, Katie spied Mrs. Simpkins walking toward them with a police officer.

"Come, Freida. Mrs. Simpkins is waiting. It's time to get some answers..."

Taking her *freind*'s arm, Katie tried to prepare herself for whatever came next.

THREE

Katie watched as Mrs. Simpkins talked to Abbott Creek's newest police officer. Katie knew the young woman had moved here a few months ago from the city, but that was all she knew about her.

The young policewoman asked lots of questions and Mrs. Simpkins answered, gesturing around the bakery as she spoke.

"What is going on, Katie?"

She turned to answer, as the worry in Freida's voice distracted her from what was going on in front of her.

"I believe Mrs. Simpkins is upset because the new policewoman told her we could not disturb anything in the bakery until they are finished with their investigation."

Freida wrung her hands as she stepped away from Katie. She paced a few steps away to the end of the sidewalk and then back.

"Of course she is upset, Katie. What are we going to do? If we are not to disturb anything, I am certain that means we cannot remove the orders that were not taken. What will we tell our customers? What will everyone take to the celebration tonight? *Ach*, Katie, why are you not more upset?"

As the police officer walked into another room, where the prepared orders were usually kept, Mrs. Simpkins turned and came near the girls, saving Katie from having to answer Freida's question.

"Girls, we're not going to be able to use anything in here. Not even the few things that were left by whoever did this. We can't use the kitchen and we can't take anything out until they're finished with their investigation."

Dear Gott, if Mrs. Simpkins hadn't needed to call the police—and the insurance company, all of this could have been avoided. We could clean everything up and get back to work.

Katie wished now she had never mentioned the police to Mrs. Simpkins. Maybe if she hadn't panicked, and mentioned calling them, Mrs. Simpkins wouldn't have gotten them involved.

It's not our way. Dat is right; their ways are not our ways. And now they are keeping us from doing our job. After all, it's not as if anyone was hurt.

"But how will we fill the customer's orders?" Freida was wringing her hands again as she spoke, quietly . . . almost to herself.

Katie looked from Mrs. Simpkins to Freida. They were only seeing the bad in this situation. Maybe there was another choice.

"We can't just wait around. We will have to find some other way to do it."

Both women turned to look at her, eyes wide. Katie scrambled for something else to say . . . some answer that must be right in front of them—only no one had seen it yet.

The rumble of a car engine drew Katie's attention to the street behind her. As she turned, the sign from the cafe across the street came into her view.

"Irish Blessings!." She said the words excitedly, thinking only of her discovery.

"The cafe?" Mrs. Simpkins and Freida asked at the same time.

"*Jah*, don't you see?"

"No." Mrs. Simpkins' response tumbled together with Freida's own "*Nee*." Katie found it a struggle not to laugh at how comical the two women sounded.

"The cafe does not open until noon. Perhaps Mr. O'Neal would let us use his kitchen to prepare our orders."

Katie stopped there, knowing full well that Mr. O'Neal would most likely do anything for Mrs. Simpkins—although she never seemed to see his affection for herself.

"*Ach*, Katie. That is a wonderful *gut* idea." Freida nearly jumped in her excitement. "We should go and ask him."

Freida looked over at Mrs. Simpkins as she spoke. When she looked back at Katie and saw the hint of a smile, she quickly put a hand up to her mouth to hide her own smile from Mrs. Simpkins.

It was true that over half the town had long speculated over whether or not anything would ever come of Andrew O'Neal's interest in Mrs. Amelia Simpkins. But so far, she seemed oblivious to it.

Perhaps there could come some *gut* from what had at first seemed like a disaster.

FOUR

Katie followed Andrew O'Neal through the swinging double doors that separated the kitchen from the dining area at the Irish Blessings, as he had affectionately named his cafe.

"It is *gut* of you to allow us to use your kitchen."

"Yes, well, um . . . your boss has a way of making it difficult for me to say no."

Katie might have worried that perhaps Mrs. Simpkins was a bit too pushy when asking their neighbor if they could use his kitchen, but she knew, even if Mrs. Simpkins had been pushy, he would have gladly done anything for her.

"I only wish I could give you more time."

Katie held her tongue for a moment, until she could think of an appropriate response. She would not have been surprised if he had chosen to close for the entire day—anything to help out Katie's boss.

"I know Mrs. Simpkins really appreciates the time you can give us. We have more than four hours to bake. That is for sure and for certain more time than we had only a few minutes ago."

He laughed before answering. "You have a point."

"And do not forget, Freida is baking at the Inn as well. *Gott* has truly blessed us in this time of hardship."

"He has, indeed." Mr. O'Neal nodded his head agreeably as they wound their way around to his supply room and pantry. "Speaking of which . . ." Mr. O'Neal gestured to the stocked shelves in the large room.

"Milly mentioned to me when we made the arrangements, that she planned to go shopping for ingredients. I know that I may not have everything you need. However, if there is something you can get started with, you are welcome to anything you can find on my shelves."

Katie ducked her head to hide her surprise. No matter how many times Mrs. Simpkins told him no one called her Milly, Mr. O'Neal always insisted on using the shortened form of her name—though more often than not, it was when he was actually speaking to her.

This was the first time Katie had heard him refer to her boss, using his nickname for her, when she was nowhere nearby to hear him.

It was just one of the ways he teased her. One of the ways he showed his affection. The affection that everyone who knew both of them saw . . . except for the lady being discussed, of course.

"*Danki*. That is mighty generous of you."

"Everything is pretty much where you would expect to find it." He gestured to the kitchen behind them.

"*Danki*." Katie said again, before going on. "I am certain I can find everything. You have a well-organized kitchen."

"Yes. Well, if there is anything else you need, just give a shout. I'll be upstairs."

"Will I need to go out front to let Mrs. Simpkins in when she arrives?"

"No, I'll buzz her in. I could have done the same when you arrived, but it seemed a better idea to show you around the kitchen."

"I appreciate that."

"All right, then. I will be going upstairs

now."

Katie watched him go, before turning back to the well-stocked pantry. Looking down at the list in her hand, she thought of the ingredients she would need for each item on the list, comparing them to what she saw on the shelves in front of her.

There were several types of cookies on the list she needed for orders that customers had scheduled to pick up early today. She should start with those.

She scanned the list again, looking for the recipes with simple ingredients. She found three different cookies she could get started on with the ingredients she had on hand.

Hmm . . . I will need flavoring for the icing . . . but for now, she could get the cookie dough started.

Katie began gathering up the supplies she would need for the three different types of cookies, carrying everything over to one of the large prep tables at the back of the spacious kitchen.

As she worked, she thought about the mess in their own kitchen. She hadn't seen much from her place by the front door of the bakery, but whether the mess had carried on into the kitchen or not, there would likely be no baking done there today.

A little while later, Katie looked up at the sound of Mrs. Simpkins' voice. "Oh good, you've already gotten a start on the orders."

Seeing how many bags her boss had in each hand, and even more looped over each arm, Katie rushed around the counter to relieve her of as many of them as possible.

"Thank you, Katie."

Mrs. Simpkins had just placed the last bag on the counter, when Mr. O'Neal walked into the kitchen behind her, similarly laden.

"My goodness, Milly! Did you buy everything in the store?"

Mrs. Simpkins only laughed and waved a hand at him in response.

She must be in a gut mood . . . not to mind his teasing.

Out loud, Katie added, "Are there more bags? And do you need help bringing them in?"

She stepped forward, starting to move around the long counter, but Mr. O'Neal put up a hand to stop her.

"You keep doing what you're doing. Neither of us can take over your job. Carrying bags . . . that we can do."

"If you're certain . . ."

"We are, Katie, but thank you." Mrs. Simpkins reached over to give Katie's hand a pat before turning to go back through the swinging doors at the kitchen's entryway.

Katie resisted looking through the bags for the moment, going back to her stirring.

She would need to get these cookies into the oven soon. Then she could go through the bags Mrs. Simpkins had brought her.

Katie spent the next two hours measuring, stirring, baking and decorating cookies and cupcakes. She put the first batch of blueberry cupcakes in the oven just as Mrs. Simpkins walked into the kitchen with Andrew O'Neal in tow.

"Katie, they're telling me now that it will be tomorrow, at the very least, before we can get back into the bakery."

"Aye, tis a good thing you made the decision to close early today, Milly." Mr. O'Neal teased, ducking out of the way when Mrs. Simpkins swiped a hand at him.

"That does nothing to help with the orders. We have customers coming to pick up their orders—and they'll find the bakery closed and nothing to pick up."

"I have good news. The police told me that most of the customer orders were left behind—untouched. They're making arrangements to bring them over to the cafe."

"Could we call the customers . . . tell them what is going on and let them know to come here or to the Inn to pick up their orders?" Katie made the suggestion hesitantly.

With everything else that was happening at the bakery, she did not want to say anything to upset her boss.

Mrs. Simpkins looked uncertain for a moment or two, but then a smile slowly bloomed on her face, making her look happier—and more relaxed, than she had looked all morning.

"Katie, that is a brilliant idea. I love it! I have everyone's contact information. I should be able to call them all."

"Should I help you?"

"No. You keep baking. I can handle calling the customers. But thank you for your wonderful suggestion."

With that, Mrs. Simpkins turned, and nearly tripped over Mr. O'Neal, as she walked toward the swinging doors at the entrance to the kitchen.

Katie stifled a laugh as the two of them made their way through the doors and into the dining area . . . Mr. O'Neal making a grand sweeping gesture with his hands, as he bent at the waist and motioned for Mrs. Simpkins to go through the doors ahead of him.

She swatted a hand at him again as she moved past, but Katie thought she could see a hint of a smile on her boss's face, as she moved through the doorway.

"Katie?"

Mrs. Simpkins called out as she came through the swinging doors, into the kitchen area.

"Katie. You've been a trooper, staying here and working all morning. Now that we have many of our orders back, and you've made enough cookies and cupcakes to cover the lost one, we're going to make all our deliveries!"

"That's wunderbaar!"

"Yes, well, that's what I want to discuss with you. We have several orders requested by families in your community. We cannot reach them by phone. Can you deliver them after you take a lunch break?"

"Of course! I would be happy to deliver them."

"All right. Then you had better get going after you eat your lunch. Mr. O'Neal has made you a sandwich to eat before you go."

"Please thank him for me. I will eat

quickly and be on my way."

"Don't rush, dear. Enjoy your meal first. Then pick up the orders. They're waiting by the side door. And you won't need to return today. Go home and get some rest before the celebration tonight."

With that, Mrs. Simpkins turned and headed back upstairs.

FIVE

A small sigh of relief escaped Katie as she stepped down from the long, wood porch. It felt wonderful *gut* knowing there were no more deliveries.

Now she would have time to go back to the cafe and clean up a bit, before Mr. O'Neal had to open for the day.

It was when she closed the gate behind her that she spotted a little *buwe*, sitting on a sagging porch next door; eating what looked like one of her specially created holiday blueberry cupcakes.

Most of the frosting was missing from the top, but the bright blue wrapper was easy to see—and Katie knew she only used those wrappers once a year.

She would not have thought anything of it, except that she knew no one had actually received an order of those cupcakes.

When she had made replacements this morning, she'd been forced to use the plain white wrappers Mrs. Simpkins had brought her.

Cautiously, she walked along the sidewalk, watching the little *buwe* as he ate the cupcake . . . a cupcake she was more and more certain had been taken from the bakery that she had found a mess this very morning.

Katie had just reached the gate that was

hanging more than a little crooked, when the little *buwe* looked up and waved.

His mouth was covered in frosting and he was as dirty as a little pig, but the smile that spread across his face was adorable and his wave was quite enthusiastic.

"Hi, there." He shouted to her when she stopped walking and returned his wave.

"Hi."

He turned away from her, only to turn back a second later. He jumped down each porch step, and once he reached the bottom, he ran over to her.

Holding out his hand to her, he asked, "Do you want one? They're really good." In his hand he held another cupcake, a bit smooshed, but otherwise untouched.

He held it up to her with another big smile, while she stood there for several seconds, trying to decide whether or not she should take it.

It had to be one of the cupcakes taken

from the bakery, but could she really accuse a *buwe* who would not be more than five years old of stealing it?

She knew she couldn't—so she decided to try and find out where it had *kumme* from . . . certainly this little *buwe* had not *kumme* all the way into town, broken into the bakery, and stolen the cupcakes.

Perhaps someone had given it to him . . .

"That cupcake does look very *gut*. Where did you get it?"

The *buwe* shrugged before answering. "I don't know where they came from, but I got it from my brothers. He brought a bunch of them home for us. They're really good."

He held it up to her again, but she was even more determined to get to the bottom of the situation than she was to take a cupcake from this little *buwe*.

"It is awfully early to be eating a cupcake. Have you had breakfast yet?"

"You talk funny. Why do you talk like

that?" He looked up at her with his head tilted to one side and a curious gleam in his eyes, but he did not answer her question.

"I am one of the plain folk. We all talk this way." She smiled at him before adding, "Maybe it is you who talks funny."

He giggled in response. "No, I don't think so. No one else I know talks that way. What are plain folk? Are they like leprechauns? The nice man who owns the restaurant in town talks funny. He says it's because he's from the island where the leprechauns live."

At that, it was Katie's turn to giggle. "*Jah*, Mr. O'Neal has some strange tales to tell, he does. *Nee*, I am not a leprechaun. Most people call us plain folk Amish."

"Oh! I've heard Mama talk about Amish people. She really likes your quilts. Papa was going to buy her one for Christmas last year, but he never got to."

Katie watched the little *buwe* in front of her as he went from happy to sad—in only a moment—and she had a strong feeling something very bad might have happened to his *dat.*

"*Jah,* our quilts are very *gut.* My *mamm* makes some of the most beautiful quilts I have ever seen. Is your *dat allrecht?*"

"He is now. He went to heaven. Mama said so. I hope she doesn't have to go there, too. I'm glad papa is better now, but I miss him. I don't want to have to miss Mama, too."

"Is your *mamm* sick?"

"Yeah. She's been awful sick for a long time. Gwen takes good care of her, but she isn't getting any better. I don't know what to do. I just hope she doesn't have to go to Heaven, too. I would miss her an awful lot."

Any thought of solving the mystery of who had broken into the bakery went right out of Katie's head, when she thought of this sweet little *buwe* losing his *dat* and maybe his *mamm,* too.

"Is your *mamm* home—or is she at the hospital?"

"Oh, she's here." He looked around before leaning in to whisper loudly, "I don't think we can afford no hospital. It costs a lot of money and we don't got any."

It was then, that Katie knew for certain, that someone in the family must have broken into the bakery, and stolen the cupcakes and bread.

The children must be hungry. And if they had *nee* money, the *bruder* he spoke of must have been desperate to find food of some kind.

Of course he broke in. If he knew they couldn't pay for anything, he might have felt he had nee other choice.

"So, your *mamm* is home—and Gwen? Is she home with your *mamm*?"

Should I ask who Gwen is? Is that a nurse . . . a relative . . . his mamm's sister?

"Is anyone else home right now?"

"Yeah. My brothers are home too . . . well, not all of my brothers. Travis is in the city. I miss him lots. He came home when we said bye to papa, but he didn't stay very long before he went away again and he never came back."

Kate realized then that there were tears in her eyes. *That won't do at all.* She blinked them away and started to think of what she could do to help them. They for sure needed help!

It took only a moment to realize she could not do enough . . . not on her own.

She would need help . . .

She would need her family . . .

She would need her *freinden* . . .

SIX

More tears fell as Katie headed home. This time she didn't even notice them; instead, her thoughts were on the little *buwe* and his family.

I can't believe it! He's been going hungry, yet he offers me one of his cupcakes!

The little *buwe* had confirmed before she left, that two of his *bruders*—not just one— had come home with bags full of bread, cookies, cupcakes, and other items.

As she walked, she struggled to come up with a way to help him—and his family. The whole family needed help—more help than she could give them.

Ach, I keep going back to that. Well, if I can't do it alone, I will have to find some help —somehow.

She knew she would ask for her family's help. But she wasn't sure how much they would help an *Englischer* family in need— after two of the *buwes* had stolen from the bakery!

And Mrs. Simpkins! What would she do when she learned of the thieves? What would this young *buwe* do if two of his *bruders* were locked up in jail! What would happen to the family?

"*Gott,* please don't let anything terrible *kumme* from this. Please watch over this family. Send others to help them—now in their time of need. Don't let their poverty cause the two *buwes* to end up in jail."

The tears were streaming down both of her cheeks, but she paid no attention to them, as she continued to pray.

"*Gott*, you know what is best for this little family. Please guide me to the ones who can help them. And *Gott*, please be with Mrs. Simpkins, when I tell her about the two *buwes*."

"*Gott*, they didn't mean to hurt anyone; I'm sure of it. They were just two desperate, little buwes! *Gott*, I trust you. I trust you to do what is best for this hurting family. And now I thank you for what you're planning for this family. I know you are planning for their *gut*."

Feeling much better after her talk with *Gott*, she dried her tears. Looking up, she was surprised to see that she was walking down the path to her own home. She had prayed all the way home!

Katie walked into the kitchen, where her *mamm* was preparing the supper to take to the town celebration.

"*Du bischt daheem*, Katie."

"*Jah, Mamm*, I am home. It has been a very busy day. And I have something I need to talk over with you. I need some help . . . with something that happened at the bakery today.

"Go ahead, Katie. Tell me what sort of help you need. What has happened that has got you so *het up*?"

"*Mamm*, You will not believe what happened today at work. When I first arrived at the bakery, the place was a mess. Not only were most of the baked goods taken, but a few of the orders we had prepared for the customers were gone, too. And the decorations in the display case were broken."

"*Ach*, Katie! I had *nee* idea something like

that could happen in our small community. I thought when we allowed you to go work in Mrs. Simpkins' bakery, it was going to be a safe place to work!"

"The only thing left behind—were the crumbs! *E*verywhere we looked there were crumbs—all over the place!" Katie looked around the room, as if she was looking for the crumbs.

"The thieves even took some of the prepared orders we had in the back, plus most of the breads and goodies in the display case."

"My goodness! I never thought something like that could happen here in our small community. I thought for certain that Mrs. Simpkins' bakery would be a safe place for you to work!

Katie stopped to pour herself a glass of water. After taking a couple of sips, she spoke again, trying to answer her *mamm's* worries.

"Mrs. Simpkins called the police and a police officer met us at the bakery. It was a *maedel*; I didn't know there were *maedel* police officers. Anyway, she came by to talk to Mrs. Simpkins and me." Katie looked a bit nervous as she looked at her *mamm*.

"Now, I know you and *dat* don't want me to talk to the police, and Mrs. Simpkins was just great. She told the police officer I didn't know anything. She insisted that I be left alone."

"Then I need to talk to Mrs. Simpkins; to thank her for this kindness to my *dochder*. Is this the help you mentioned?"

"*Nee*, *Mamm*. The help I need is with the thieves!"

"Katie, I'm for sure and for certain glad that you didn't get into any troubling situation, but what are you thinking— needing help with some thieves."

"But *Mamm*, it's not like it sounds. It was only an accident that I found out who the thieves are. I had just delivered the last order this afternoon, when I saw a young *buwe* eating a blueberry cupcake—one that I had baked yesterday, using bright blue wrappers."

"Well, for mercy sakes. And he is one of the thieves?"

"*Nee, Mamm*. He has two older *bruders* who must have stolen all the food they could carry, I suppose. And now I don't know how to tell Mrs. Simpkins. I'm for sure hoping that she won't press charges. After all, they were starving. Otherwise, I'm certain they wouldn't have done it. I'm thinking that you and *dat* should go by and talk to the children —and their *mamm*."

"Whatever for? Why would we want to interfere? Is the family part of the community—are they plain?"

"No, *Mamm*. They are *Englischers*. But the *dat* has passed on, and the *mamm* is sick. I don't for sure know how the children are getting by. If they have *nee* money for food, it's *nee* wonder the little ones are sneaking into town to steal. Now I'm knowing that they need to be told how wrong that is . . . but they are for sure needing our help."

Soon after Katie had explained everything to her *mamm*, they had come up with a plan—of sorts. First, Katie boxed up some of the foodstuffs they had in their cellar, while her *mamm* picked out a couple of pretty quilts for the family.

While Katie headed back to town, her *mamm* took herself over to her nearest neighbor's farm. If these people needed help, it would take more than one family.

Martha would talk to the Bishop's *frau*, who would get some of the other families involved. The community would rally together and see to the needs of this family, whether it was food, or clothes, or financial obligations. And the oldest *buwe* . . . someone would contact him to come back home—to help out with his family.

Whatever this family needed, Martha knew they needed the help of their neighbors...

SEVEN

The bell over the cafe's door clanged madly as Katie hurriedly rushed through it.

Mr. O'Neal will know how to help me tell Mrs. Simpkins what is going on.

Katie had left her *mamm* boxing up more food.

She had *kumme* back to town to speak with Mrs. Simpkins about the family, but she was hoping to have some help with her explanation.

She knew what the children had done was not a *gut* thing, but with the police already involved, she was hoping Mr. O'Neal could help keep Mrs. Simpkins from making their situation even worse.

"Katie, what's your hurry?"

"I need your help. I have to go and speak to Mrs. Simpkins and I am mighty worried about how she is going to react to what I have to tell her."

"All right then, why don'cha tell me first and then we can go speak with her together."

"*Allrecht.* This afternoon I found out who broke into the bakery."

"Now that's something I didn't expect you to say . . . you really found the thieves?"

"*Jah.* I really found them. At least I found out who they are. I didn't actually meet them —or see them, but there is *nee* doubt that they are the thieves."

"And I'm guessing there's a lot more to

that story, then?"

"*Jah*, definitely more to the story."

"Out with it, then."

Katie told him everything she knew—from finding the little *buwe*, to what he had told her, and finally, to what her *mamm* and their neighbors were doing right this minute.

He sat attentively, listening to everything she said, before asking any questions.

"And he told you his brother is in the city. Did he say where? Which city?"

"*Nee*, and I didn't think to ask him."

"It's all right, Katie. It isn't as if we can't go back and talk to him again. We'll get the information we need."

"*Jah*." Katie thought again about the little *buwe*. The thought of going back to his house made her excited, but sad.

Excited because she knew she could help him now. Sad because she truly didn't know how Mrs. Simpkins would take the news of the thieves.

Would she be angry? Would she insist the police arrest those *buwes*?

Katie really hoped she would not.

How old are they?

They have to be young buwes. If they were old enough to work, they wouldn't have stolen food to feed their family.

Mr. O'Neal interrupted her thoughts.

"Here is what I'm thinkin'. Your *mam* is putting together some things to take over to the family?"

"*Jah,* she and a few of her *freinden.*"

"So, we have a reason to go over there again. We'll talk to them . . . find out a bit more about what it is that's goin' on with them."

"Should we invite Mrs. Simpkins to go along with us, then?"

"Absolutely. That's part of my plan. I believe Milly would benefit from seeing the situation for herself. Don'cha think so?"

"*Jah.* It's a *gut* idea."

He answered with a nod. "All right then, let's go get Milly. I'll drive."

Andrew stopped his vehicle several houses away from their destination. He looked over at Milly and then back at Katie.

Milly was stoic, calm, no hint of how or what she was feeling, but Katie—well, she had concern all over her features.

There were three vehicles in front of the small house—two police cruisers and a small, slightly beat-up car that reminded him of his first car back in Ireland.

"Looks like we don't have to worry about informing the police."

"Shush you." Milly responded quickly—bringing a smile to Andrew's face.

"Well, let's go and see what we can do about all of this."

He reached for his door handle—and

before he could even pull it, Milly was out of the car and on the sidewalk.

He looked down and shook his head, feeling a wry smile spread across his face before he opened his door and stepped out.

Katie had climbed out of the back and turned to close the car door as he rounded the hood, so he nodded at them both and turned toward the house.

EIGHT

Katie walked along the path to the little *buwe's* house. The stones under her feet might be old, worn—even cracked and crumbling—but they were clean and the yard around them was well-maintained.

With *nee* little *buwe* to distract her, she took the time to look over it a bit more. It was in need of a fresh coat of paint, but it appeared clean.

There were a few toys strewn about the porch area, but *nee* mess or clutter to be seen. If it weren't for the car sitting in the driveway and the power line running to a pole attached to the house, it might have been one of her plain neighbor's homes.

She looked over at Mr. O'Neal and Mrs. Simpkins before reaching up to knock on the door. They both nodded, so she went ahead.

The door was opened by a waif of a girl after only a moment or two. She peered up at them from inside a darkened room, but said nothing.

Katie looked into the room—over the girl's head—at the sound of several deep voices. The girl flinched a little when one of the voices sounded louder than the others.

"Is your mother home?" Mrs. Simpkins said, from behind Katie.

"She is . . . but . . ." The girl turned to look behind her and then turned back to them. "She's not available at the moment."

"Is she speaking to the police?"

The girl didn't answer, but Katie took her frightened expression for a yes.

"Please, we need to come in and speak with your mother." Andrew added from behind her.

"Is that the lady who talks so pretty?" The young *buwe,* who she'd spoken to before, peeked around the door, taking hold of it with both hands.

"Bobby, Travis said not to let anyone else in."

"But Gwen, she's my friend. I'm sure Travis didn't mean she couldn't come in."

"Fine, but I'm not taking the blame." With that she backed away from the door—which the young *buwe* swung all the way open.

"Come on in."

"*Danki.*" Bobby—now she knew his name--giggled at her word and she couldn't help smiling back at him.

He took hold of her hand and pulled her with him, through the house, to a hall with several doors leading off of it.

He stopped at the end of the hall, in front of a doorway. Through it, Katie could see two police officers, the police chief, who was a very tall, thin middle-aged man, two young *buwes* who could not have been any older than her two *bruders* and a very pale older woman lying in bed, blankets tucked carefully all around her.

No one was paying any attention to them. Most of the attention in the room was on the trio of police officers and the tall young man who Katie thought must be Travis.

She had a moment to wonder who had called him . . . and why they had not called him before they were starving and forced to steal, but she pushed that thought away, recognizing how uncharitable it was.

It is not my place to judge anyone.

One of the police officers shifted and

Katie could see that it was the same woman who had *kumme* to the bakery that morning.

That makes sense, I suppose.

Katie watched as the young man argued with the police officers—and since his young *bruder* made *nee* attempt to pull Katie into the room, she was content to stand outside the doorway . . . as far away from the arguing as possible.

However, Mrs. Simpkins chose that moment to speak up. She moved past Katie and walked into the room, right up to the group.

As she did, all conversation stopped. Everyone looked around at each other. Then the policewoman spoke up.

"Ah, good. Sir, Mrs. Simpkins here is the owner of the bakery in question." She gestured first to the police chief, and then to Katie's boss.

As soon as she mentioned the bakery, a deep, red stain crept up the young man's face and he stepped back a little. Then he turned to aim a fierce glare at his younger *bruders*.

Katie watched all of it, praying *Gott* would keep His hand on the situation, guiding everyone to the best possible solution . . . though Katie had absolutely *nee* idea what that could possibly be.

"So, Mrs. Simpkins, we've been talking with this young man." And he gestured beside him to Travis. "He informed us that his younger brothers have confessed to him that they did indeed break into your shop this morning and steal quite a lot of bread and other sweets."

The young man spoke up. "Yes, but Officer, you must realize the situation was dire. They were starving. They had no idea what else to do."

"Yes, you said that before. What I don't understand is what you intend on doing about it. Why are you so certain the situation will not continue to be dire?"

"Because I am home now. I'll take care of things. And I will make sure this doesn't happen again." He aimed another fierce look at his *bruders*.

"And why is it that you were not here to begin with? Why did you not check on your family?"

"Because I didn't know how serious the situation was. When my brothers broke into the bakery, Gwen called me. I got here as quickly as I could. I didn't even pack my things."

The police chief turned to look at the group still standing in the doorway. "And why didn't you call him before now? With your mother so sick, and no one taking care of you . . . were you too busy enjoying the freedom?"

Katie looked around her, trying to figure out who the man was speaking to—and realized that he must be speaking to the young girl who had answered the door.

She must have followed them down the hall, but Katie had not heard anything to give away her approach.

"Mama told me not to." The young woman spoke very quietly, but Katie could hear the anguish in her voice.

Clearly she was only concerned for her brothers and what their punishment would be. Katie watched as she stood there, twisting her hands together and shifting from foot to foot as she waited for more questions from the police chief.

However, he turned his attention back to Travis. "Let me see if I have this right. Six months ago, your father died—and instead of staying home to take care of your family, you go off to the city."

Katie felt bad for Travis, but he stood still and listened quietly as the officer continued.

"You only come back when your younger brothers break into a bakery—and you expect me to believe that it won't happen again, that you won't head right back to the city when I leave here? Is that about right?"

"Officer,"

"Chief."

"I'm sorry, Chief . . . I promise you, I did not run out on my family. I had no idea mom was sick. She was the one who told me to go to the city. I've been sending money home from every paycheck."

"Obviously, it was not enough." He said this in an undertone, to himself, before he went on.

"Now that I know what is going on, I will not be going back to the city. I mean, I will, but only to get my things. I will be moving back home to take care of things."

The police chief turned to Katie's boss then. "Well, there you have it, Mrs. Simpkins. What do you want to do with them?"

NINE

Mrs. Simpkins looked from Travis, to his younger brothers, who were huddled together on the couch behind him, to their mother on the bed in the corner of the room, to the young woman who had moved to her side, and then to Katie—and the young boy still holding tightly to her hand.

"I do not wish to press charges." She turned to look at the two boys on the couch and continued. "I will expect the two of you to clean up your mess."

After a moment, she added, "First thing in the morning."

Both boys nodded enthusiastically in answer. Travis spoke up as well. "And I can pay you for the things they took."

But Mrs. Simpkins was shaking her head. "No, I think it's more important to use your money to care for your mother—and your brothers and sister."

"I don't want them to feel like they can get away with anything." Travis looked back over at his brothers, but Mrs. Simpkins spoke up again.

"They aren't getting away with anything. They made a mess and they are going to make it right. And by saving me the money it would cost to hire a special clean-up crew, they are paying me back for the things they took."

Amelia glanced over to see Katie watching her and the stubborn young man— who continued to stand there with his arms crossed over his chest.

"I don't know about you boys, but I would take that deal." The gruff police chief spoke up then.

Travis opened his mouth, but Mrs. Simpkins shook her head at him. "I understand what you're concerned about, but it was my shop that was broken into and I say this is the way we are going to handle it."

She put up a hand when he opened his mouth again. "I've made up my mind and that is just how it's going to be. Don't waste your breath arguing with me."

Travis finally unfolded his arms and then raised them in a gesture of defeat. "Okay. You win. We'll do it your way." He looked at his brothers again before adding, "for now anyway."

Mrs. Simpkins nodded her head and then turned to the police officers.

"Is there anything else—or is that all?"

"There's nothing else to it, ma'am. You've taken care of everything." The police chief answered, with one last withering stare at young Travis.

"You've been given a second chance. I don't want to see any of you in trouble again . . . understand me?"

Every child in the room nodded, even the young boy still clinging so tightly to Katie—though he had moved behind her skirts.

Amelia hadn't noticed earlier, but now—looking over at him—she could just barely see his head peeking around Katie's side.

Katie reached down to him, rubbing a hand on his back, trying to reassure him.

"Guess we'll be going now." The police chief spoke up again, clearing his throat loudly and then looking around the room one more time before moving toward the door.

Katie stepped into the room and out of the man's path, ducking her head a little as he and his deputies passed.

Gwen, the young girl, slipped quietly behind them, following them toward the front door. Young Bobby let go of Katie's skirt as soon as his sister moved past them.

Katie watched him bound across the room to his mother's bedside. He pulled himself up on her bed and sat there, playing with the blanket that was wrapped so tightly around her. Katie watched him for several seconds, until Mrs. Simpkins' voice drew her attention.

"No, now I told you I want you to use that to take care of your family. I guarantee they need it more than I do."

Evidently, the young man had tried again

to pay her for the items his *bruders* had taken from her bakery.

Katie hid a smile, knowing exactly how difficult it was to talk her boss out of—or into—anything.

"You just be certain the boys are there bright and early tomorrow morning. We open at seven, so they'll need to be there at least a half hour before, I would think."

"We'll be there, ma'am. Thank you."

"Well, now that it's all settled, there's a celebration to get to. If we hurry, we might even get there before the food is gone." Mr. O'Neal stepped up to stand beside Mrs. Simpkins as he spoke.

"I don't think we'll be going." Travis said, just as his *schweschder* came back into the room.

And for the first time since they had all *kumme* into the room, Katie heard their *mamm's* voice.

"Nonsense. We always go to the Fourth of

July celebration. Travis, you take your brothers and sister and get down there to celebrate. I mean it!" Her voice was very small and sounded weak, but there was a firm determination to it that made it impossible to consider arguing.

Katie recognized it as a tone her own *mamm* used often. She was not at all surprised to hear Travis mumble "yes, ma'am" in response.

"You all go on. I'll stay with Mama." Gwen spoke quietly, but Katie heard her.

And apparently Mrs. Simpkins did, too.

"You will do no such thing, young lady. Your mama just told your brother to take you to the festivities and that is what he's going to do."

"I can't. Someone has to stay with Mama."

"Yes, I know. This why I am going to stay here."

"But . . ."

"No buts, now you go get ready. I have been to that same festival every year since my dear late husband moved us here. And I am sure the year will come when you have to miss one, but it is not going to be this year."

She made a little scooting motion with her hands as she walked over to the bed in the corner. "Go on now."

That time she made the motion to Travis, who was still standing at the foot of his *mamm's* bed.

He didn't hesitate that time. He took his young *bruder's* hand and headed for the door, his other two *bruders* following right behind him.

His *schweschder* looked over at her *mamm*—who nodded her head at her daughter—and then she followed her *bruders* out.

"Katie, will you be certain Freida has delivered the cupcakes to the park?"

"Yes, Mrs. Simpkins. I sure will."

"All right. Off with you, too. Now go have fun."

"Are you certain you don't need help here?"

"I sat by my husband's sick bed many a time in my life. I will be just fine."

Looking over at the children's *mamm*, Amelia smiled. "Now then, I think it's time for introductions, don't you?" Amelia sat down beside the bed.

"I'm Amelia Simpkins. You already know that I own The Sweet Shop in town. And this silly man who insists on calling me Milly is Andrew O'Neal. He owns a cafe in town."

"And I'm Cissy Davis. I'm sorry that I can't get up right now, but I've been recovering from—"

"Now, you don't need to say any more. We'll have a nice chat after everyone leaves."

"Come on, Katie. Looks like Milly has things handled."

Amelia scowled at Andrew, but said

nothing about his usage of the nickname she detested.

He only smiled and turned to walk back down the hall toward the front door.

—— EPILOGUE ——

K atie could hardly believe everything that had happened today. It had started out so ordinary; then she had discovered the mess before the day had even begun.

At the time, she would never have believed that not only would the bakery have been broken into, but that the *buwes* involved—and their family, would become *freinden* of her own family!

Katie looked around at her *freinden* and neighbors as she walked toward the center of the park, surrounded by her family.

In her hands, she carried a large plastic box filled with cupcakes. She spied Freida on the other side of the park, who was similarly laden with her own box of cupcakes, walking with her own family.

Behind Katie, her *mamm* had the third box of cupcakes, while her *dat* carried the box of food her family was contributing to the town picnic.

Her *schweschders* walked beside her and *mamm,* while their *bruders* ran ahead, in a rush to put down the things they were carrying so they could find their *freinden.*

When they got close to the center of the park, where a dozen long picnic tables waited—some already weighed down with piles of food and supplies—Katie spotted Travis with his *bruders* and *schweschder.*

Just like her *bruders*, his were running

around, playing with their own *freinden*, shouting happily. They all looked happy to be there.

Katie laughed as she walked over to one of the center tables—where Mr. O'Neal was arranging the large, white tablecloth Mrs. Simpkins used for special displays.

"Don'cha be worrying yourself, Katie-girl. The two of them were gettin' along like old chums when I left 'em."

"Actually, I wasn't worrying. I was thinking how glad I am at how this all worked out. *Gott* has truly been working here."

"Oh, aye, that He has. God certainly works in mysterious ways. Even if we don't understand the why's and wherefore's"

Katie smiled at that. *Who would have ever thought we would have been robbed—and then, when we found the thieves, instead of putting them in jail, we helped them. We found a family—a neighbor—instead of an enemy.* To Mr. O'Neal, she only said, "He does, indeed."

After putting down her box of cupcakes, she turned to look out at the park. Freida was talking to one of the Yoder *buwes.*

No surprise there...

Katie's *bruders* were chasing the two *buwes* who had caused so much trouble this morning.

Their *schweschder,* looking shy, was standing by the duck pond, all on her own, her face lifted to the sky in what looked to Katie like an expression of worship.

While Katie stood watching, the young woman turned to look over at the *buwes* standing on the other side of the Yoder *buwe* that Freida was talking to.

She was very far away, and Katie couldn't be certain, but it looked as if there was a shy smile playing around the young *maedel's* lips.

Intrigued, she turned back to the table.

"Do you need help with these?"

"No, Katie, you go enjoy yourself."

Katie nodded and headed off to the pond, thinking she might invite the young *maedel* to join them for the fireworks.

Gott is gut.

Blessed is he whose transgression
is forgiven, whose sin is covered.
Psalm 32:1

TURN THE PAGE

FOR EXCLUSIVE

BONUS CONTENT

DISCUSSION QUESTIONS

WARNING : SPOILERS AHEAD!

1) In the same situation as Katie, would you have responded the way she did – not only extending grace, but gathering food and supplies for the family?

2) Do you think the boys should have received a harsher punishment for what they did? Why or why not?

3) How would you react to the discovery that your home or business had been broken into, burglarized and trashed?

4) Did you expect the outcome . . . Mrs. Simpkins reaction? Why or why not?

5) In your opinion, is it easier to forgive someone you love . . . or is it easier to extend forgiveness to a complete stranger?

BLUEBERRY CUPCAKES

RECIPE CONTRIBUTED BY DJ MYNATT

INGREDIENTS:

1 white or yellow cake mix
2 cups fresh blueberries
3 eggs
1/3 cup oil
1 1/3 cups water

Prepare cake mix according to directions. Add 2 cups fresh blueberries and fold into batter. Bake following instructions on cake mix box.

ICING:

1 cup confectioner's sugar
2 tbsp. Milk
additional milk as needed

Prepare icing, mixing small amounts of confectioners sugar with milk to desired consistency. Spread onto cooled cupcakes.

Recipe © DJMynatt 2016

AUTHOR INTERVIEW

Q: What inspired you to write Amish cozy mysteries? Is there another genre you enjoy writing – or would enjoy giving a try at some point in your career?

A: My favorite genre is Amish fiction, but it wasn't the first genre I chose when I began writing – my first novel was a contemporary romance. However, it seems to be the genre I feel led to write about now. And yes, there's a back-story there (see the next question/answer).

Q: Is there something specific that led you to write this particular series? Why a Sweet Shop? Why Amish? Why a cozy mystery – and not suspense?

A: I felt compelled – urged – to stop and write an Amish cozy mystery. A Sweet Shop brings visions of pastries, cakes, things we love. Why Amish? Because most (not all, unfortunately) Amish stories are clean reads, without bad language, bad habits, and an indecent style of living. I stopped writing an Amish suspense and switched to a cozy mystery, because I think people need stories of hope and love right now. This is what I'm writing . . . a light mystery with a happy ending. Something that shows the good in people.

Q: Will there be more books in the series?

A: Oh, yes. I'm working on book two now, titled *Christmas Cookie Mystery*. If all goes well, next year the third book should be released.

Q: Can we look forward to more books from you – beyond this series?

A: I certainly hope so. I have every intention of submitting the Amish suspense novel I wrote, titled *Plain Intent*, in the future. And if people enjoy the cozy mysteries, I hope to write many more . . . and other series in the same strain.

Q: Do you have any advice for novice or debut authors?

A: Don't give up – no matter what! If you love to write, you should be writing.

ABOUT THE AUTHOR

Naomi Miller mixes up a batch of intrigue, sprinkled with Amish, Mennonite, and English characters, adding a pinch of mystery – and a dash of romance!

Naomi works full time as an author, blogger and inspirational speaker. She is a member of the American Christian Fiction Writers (ACFW) organization. When she's not working diligently to finish the next novel in her Sweet Shop Mystery series, Naomi tries to make time for attending workshops and writers conferences. Whenever time permits, Naomi can be found in one of two favorite places – the beach and the mountains.

Naomi's day is spent focusing on her writing, editing, and blogging about her experiences. Naomi loves traveling with her family, singing inspirational/gospel music, taking a daily walk, and witnessing to others of the amazing grace of Jesus Christ.

DON'T MISS THE NEXT BOOK IN THIS SERIES – COMING SOON!

AMISH SWEET SHOP
MYSTERY

Christmas Cookie
MYSTERY

NAOMI MILLER

ABOUT THE PUBLISHER

CHRISTIAN PUBLISHING FOR HIS GLORY

S&G Publishing offers books with messages that honor Jesus Christ to the world! S&G works with Christian authors to bring you the best in "inspirational" fiction and non-fiction.

S&G is proud to publish a variety of Christian fiction genres:
inspirational romance
young reader
young adult
speculative
historical
suspense

Check out our website at

sgpublish.com

JUNIOR AUTHOR SERIES

JUNIOR AUTHOR SERIES

My Dolphin Friends

GWENDOLYN MILLER

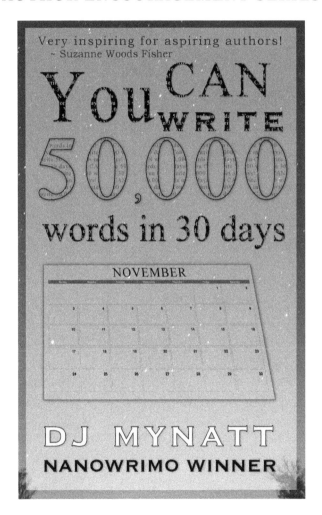

Very inspiring for aspiring authors!
~ Suzanne Woods Fisher

You CAN WRITE
50,000
words in 30 days

NOVEMBER

DJ MYNATT
NANOWRIMO WINNER

A RELUCTANT ASSASSIN

~ ORDER OF THE MOONSTONE ~

JC MORROWS

A Treacherous Decision

~ ORDER OF THE MOONSTONE ~

JC MORROWS

A DESPERATE ESCAPE

~ ORDER OF THE MOONSTONE ~

JC MORROWS

COMING SOON FROM S&G

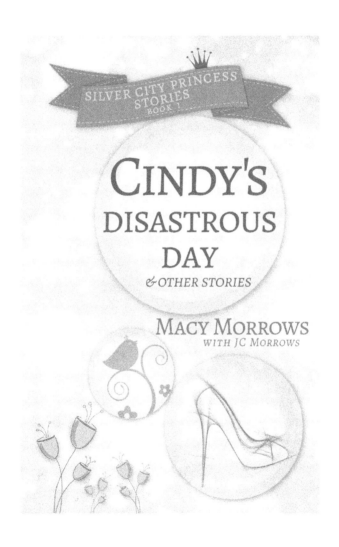

SILVER CITY PRINCESS STORIES
BOOK 1

CINDY'S DISASTROUS DAY

& OTHER STORIES

MACY MORROWS
WITH JC MORROWS

CPSIA information can be obtained
at www.ICGtesting.com
Printed in the USA
LVHW011701020620
657245LV00014B/1631